Pirates
in the
Supermarket

Blackbeard

Slim Jim

Red Ruby

Seasick Susan

Squirt

To Felix, Jamie and Harper, with love
T.K.

For Lucy and Harry
and all the trips to gaze at the fish counter
S.W.

First published in 2017 by Scholastic Children's Books
Euston House, 24 Eversholt Street
London NW1 1DB
a division of Scholastic Ltd
www.scholastic.co.uk
London ~ New York ~ Toronto ~ Sydney ~ Auckland
Mexico City ~ New Delhi ~ Hong Kong

Pirates
in the
Supermarket

By Timothy Knapman

Illustrated by Sarah Warburton

SCHOLASTIC

Pirates don't go shopping –
They are not like Mum and me.
They steal and sail and fight and roar.
They never leave the sea!

But then I take a look around
And who's here? Can you guess?

It's a mob of **naughty** pirates
Making the most dreadful mess!

Blackbeard, swinging on a rope,
Sprays ketchup in the air.

While Hooky opens cans of fizz
That fountain everywhere!

There are pirates in the supermarket!
Look, you'll see them too!
I tell my mum but she replies,
"Now don't be silly, you!"

So Eyepatch digs a great big hole,
And no one says, "Do not!"
He buries his huge treasure chest
Right where **eggs** mark the spot!

But the grown-ups keep on shopping
As if it's all okay!
They're busy and don't see them
Or hear me when I say:

"There's an anchor
in the butter!"

There's a spyglass by the juice!

There are parrots on the carrots!

There are PIRATES on the loose!"

The check-out staff say, "Pirates?
We don't have them any more!"

"But who's this lot," I ask them,
"Wheeling cannons through your store?"

"Help!" they cry.
"It's pirates!
We've made a big mistake!"

The pirates grin — and start to fill
Their cannons up with cake!

KERSPLUFFLE!

"Oh no!" the staff all scream,
As the pirates cover them
In icing, crumbs and cream.

I make a hat from boxes and
A cutlass out of bread.
I say, "I'm Captain Crossbones —
The man all pirates dread!

So get this whole shop shipshape,
Or I'll make you walk the plank,
And when the sharks are nibbling you
It's me they'll have to thank!"

Those seadogs set to scrubbing
Till the supermarket's clean.
It ends up looking like a place
No pirate's ever been.

They run off to their pirate ship.
They **swear** they won't come back.
But I'm not sure I trust them —
They might try a new attack.

So when you're in a supermarket
Keep a lookout, do.
Those **pirates** might be hiding
Not so very far from you!

Blackbeard

Slim Jim

Red Ruby

Seasick Susan

Squirt